THE
RUGRATS
MOVIE ™

Tommy's New Playmate

by Luke David
illustrated by John Kurtz and Sandrina Kurtz

Simon Spotlight/Nickelodeon

Rugrats created by Arlene Klasky, Gabor Csupo, and Paul Germain

SIMON SPOTLIGHT
An imprint of Simon & Schuster Children's Publishing Division
1230 Avenue of the Americas
New York, New York 10020

Manufactured in the United States of America

First Edition   10 9 8 7 6 5 4 3

ISBN 0-689-82141-7

The Pickleses were holding a baby shower at their home. A lot of people were in the backyard. One table was piled high with presents and another was loaded with delicious sweets.

Chuckie was amazed at all the noise and activity. He asked his best friend Tommy, "Did your baby sister finally come?"

"Not yet," Tommy answered. "But they're giving her this big party, so I'm pretty sure today's the day!"

Tommy's Grandma Minka took Didi's hand and led her through the crowd. "Come Didila! Look what we got for you!"

Tommy, Chuckie, Phil, and Lil followed close behind. Grandpa Boris led out a goat on a leash. Grandma Minka explained, "Nothing better for the little bubbala than goat's milk!"

"Except maybe yak's, but you try finding a good yak these days!" added Grandpa Boris.

"Maaaaaaa!" bleated the goat. Chuckie jumped back, startled. Grandpa Boris laughed, "The goat's just saying hello! Here you go, *kinderlach*!" He gave each baby a handful of chocolate coins.

Tommy and his friends slipped beneath a table to eat their chocolates. They gobbled them all up, except for one. Tommy held the last coin in his hand.

"Aren't you going to eat it?" asked Phil.

"Nope," answered Tommy. "I'm saving it for my baby sister!"

"Oh, you mean she finally came?" asked Chuckie, looking around.

"I don't see her, Tommy. Do ya think she got losted on her way to the party?" asked Phil.

"Hmm," said Tommy. "I don't know. Maybe we'd better go look for her!"

"But she could be anywheres!" wailed Chuckie.

The kids headed to Tommy's room. Inside they found a brand-new bed for Tommy. Nearby was Tommy's old crib, which would now belong to Tommy's new baby sister. Half the room had been painted in pink.

"Tommy, somebody's been coloring your room!" said Chuckie.

"Yep," said Tommy, "it's for my new sister."

"How are we going to find her when we don't even know what she looks like?" asked Phil.

"Well, she's a girl like me," answered Lil, "so we know she'll be prettyful!"

At that moment Angelica burst in. "Out of my way, you dumb babies!" She dumped some cookies on the bed, which was already overflowing with sweets.

"Angelica, can you help us find my baby sister?" asked Tommy.

"I wouldn't be in such a big hurry if I was you, Tommy," Angelica responded. "When the new baby gets here, she's gonna get all the toys and the love and attention, and your mommy and daddy'll forget all about you!"

"My mommy and daddy won't forget me!" said Tommy.

"That's what Spike said before you were born . . . back when his name was Paul." Angelica gave Tommy a mean look. "When you came along they put him out in the rain and he turned into a dog."

"But that's not gonna happen to me, Angelica. My mommy and daddy'll love me, no matter what!" said Tommy.

Suddenly they heard someone singing in the backyard.

Angelica rushed to the window. "Who does Susie Carmichael think she is?" she yelled as she ran out.

The kids hurried to the backyard after Angelica. She joined Susie, and together they started singing "A Baby Is a Gift From a Bob."

During the song, Chuckie said to Tommy, "Do you really think babies are a gift from a Bob, Tommy? 'Cause if Bob bringed a gift, it's probably one of them," he said, pointing to the shower gifts on the table.

Chuckie, Tommy, Phil, and Lil crawled over and started ripping wrapping paper off the gifts.

As Angelica and Susie were finishing their song, Tommy opened the last present. No baby!

Just then Angelica and Susie hit their last, particularly horrible note. Suddenly Tommy's mom gasped. She hugged her giant belly. Her face squinched up in pain.

"Oh, Betty!" Didi said to her best friend. "It's time!"

At that very moment, the goat got loose and knocked over a table. The table hit a sprinkler valve, which turned on all the sprinklers. People zigzagged away from the spray, trying not to get soaked.

Grandpa Lou scooped Tommy up and said, "Now that's what I call a baby shower!"

Didi was rushed to the Lipschitz Birthing Center. In the corridor, she held Tommy's hand. "Don't worry, Sweetie. Mommy's going to be okay."

Tommy's dad, Stu, pushed her away in a wheelchair behind the doctor.

"Gosh, Tommy," said Chuckie, "your mommy sure seems upset."

"Maybe your baby sister really is losted!" said Lil.

Tommy replied, "Well, maybe we can buy a new one." He pulled the last chocolate coin from his diaper. "Let's go find my new sister!"

The grandpas didn't notice the kids walking away down the hall.

"Waaaah! Waaaah!" Crying came from behind some big doors. Tommy pushed them open.

"Hey," said Phil, "a baby store!"
"You guys! Help me pick one my mom will like," said Tommy.

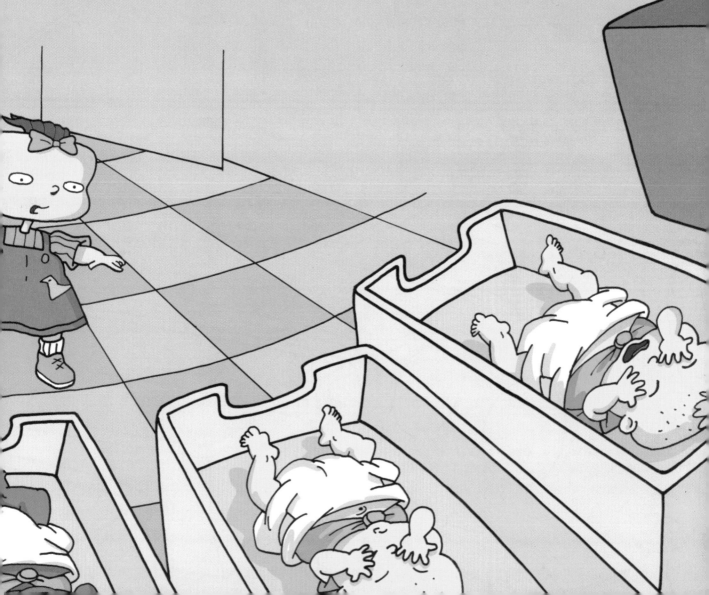

Tommy, Chuckie, Phil, and Lil moved from one tiny wrinkled baby to the next as the newborns sang "This World Is Something New to Me."

Meanwhile Didi and Stu were in the delivery room. The doctor was holding the just-born baby.

Stu looked at the tiny baby. "She's so beautiful, Didi! She's so precious! She's . . . she's a boy!" he exclaimed.

"Hello, my wonderful, sweet baby boy," said Didi as she took him in her arms.

"I guess we won't be naming him Trixie," said Stu. Instead they named him Dylan. "Dil for short. Dil Pickles," said Stu. "I like it."

After the grandpas found Tommy and his friends in the nursery, they took them to Didi's room. Didi was in bed, and all around her stood her family and friends.

Grandpa Lou put Tommy on the bed next to the new baby.

"Tommy," Didi said, "I want you to meet someone very special. This is your brother Dil."

Tommy was suddenly filled with happiness. He smiled at his new brother and reached out his hand to touch him. At that moment Baby Dil began to wail. He grabbed Tommy's nose with all his strength.

"Ow-wee!" yelled Tommy.

Even though Tommy's nose hurt, he decided to keep Baby Dil. He paid the nurse with his last chocolate coin.

Didi hugged her two boys. "See," she whispered to Stu, "they already love each other."